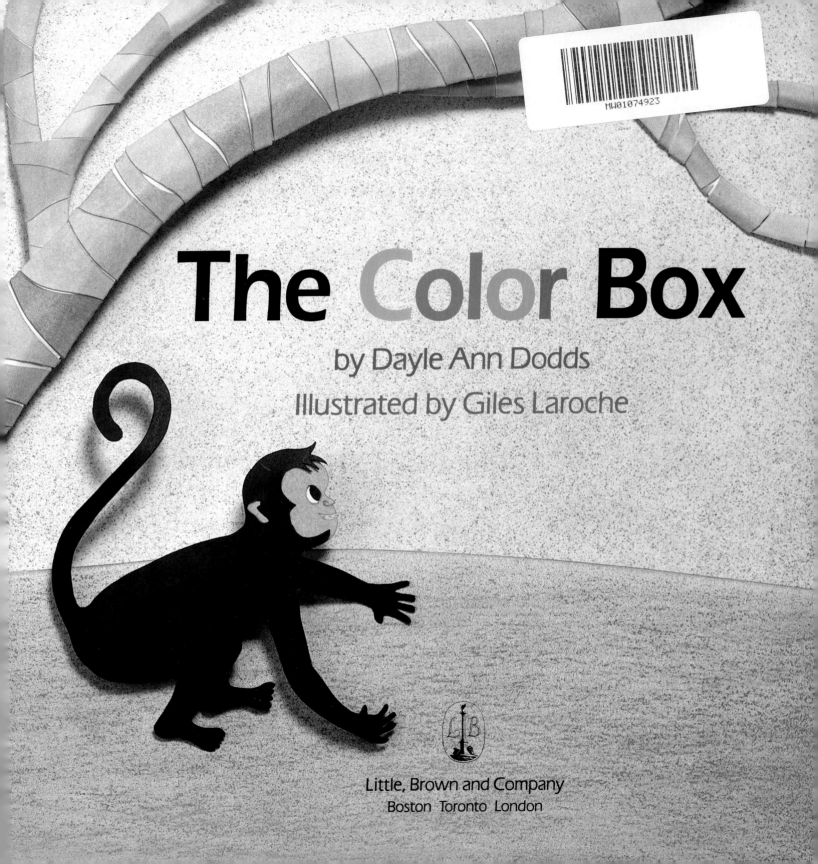

The Color Box

by Dayle Ann Dodds

Illustrated by Giles Laroche

Little, Brown and Company

Boston Toronto London

One day Alexander found a funny-looking box.

He peeked inside
And crawled inside.

It was black,
Black, *everywhere* —
Everywhere he looked.

Only one spot
Was not.
Alexander peered through
And climbed through.
What did he find?

Yellow daisies,

Yellow bees,

Yellow bananas up in trees.

Yellow, yellow, *everywhere* —
Everywhere he looked.
But then
He looked again.

He saw a ^{high} spot.
And yellow it was not.

Alexander pulled himself up
And dropped down.
What did he find?

Orange pails,

Orange sun,

Orange hats just for fun.

Orange, orange, *everywhere*—
Everywhere he looked.
But then
He looked again.

He saw a low spot.
And orange it was not.
He touched the spot.

Wet!

Alexander dove in
And splashed out.
What did he find?

Blue sky,

Blue sea,

Blue dolphins, 1, 2, 3.

Blue, blue, *everywhere* —
Everywhere he looked.
But then
He looked again.

He saw a tiny spot.
And blue it was not.

Alexander squeezed through
And popped out.
What did he find?

Red apples,

Red roses,

Circus clowns with red noses.

Red, red, *everywhere* —
Everywhere he looked.
But then
He looked again.

He saw a GREAT BIG spot.
And red it was not.

Alexander jumped in
And jumped out.
What did he find?

Green leaves,

Green frogs,

Green lizards under logs.

Green, green, *everywhere* —
Everywhere he looked.
But then
He looked again.

He saw a squiggly spot.
And green it was not.

So Alexander wiggled in
And wiggled out.
What did he find?

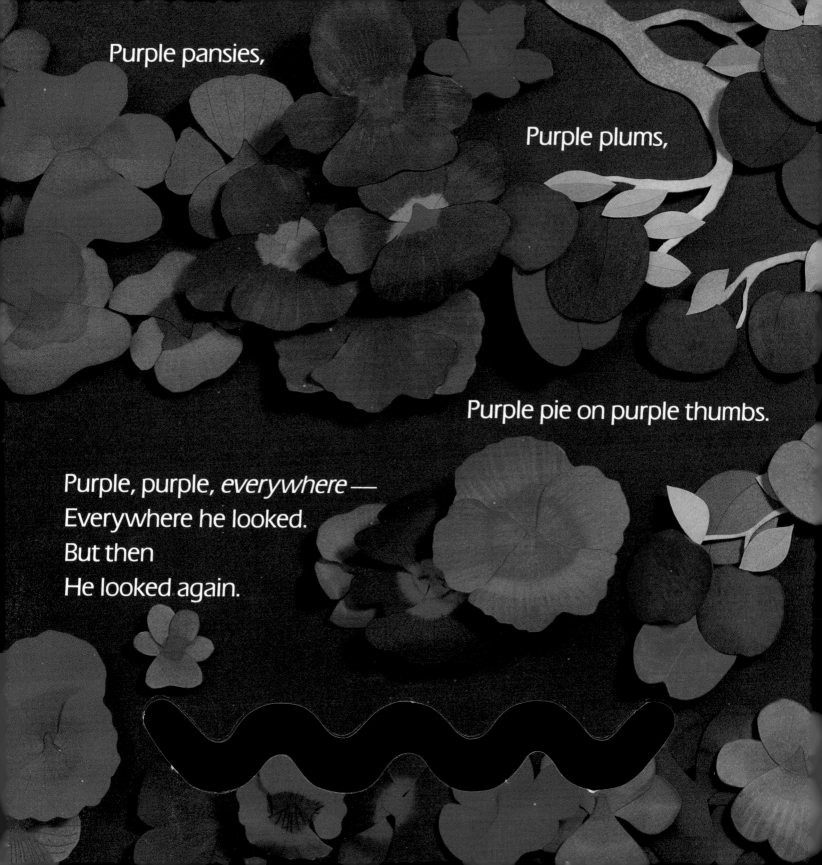

Purple pansies,

Purple plums,

Purple pie on purple thumbs.

Purple, purple, *everywhere* —
Everywhere he looked.
But then
He looked again.

He saw a skinny spot.
And purple it was not.

Alexander slipped through
And slid down.
What did he find?

White snowflakes,

A white bunny,

White snowmen looking funny.

White, white, *everywhere* —
Everywhere he looked.

Alexander searched high.

Alexander searched low.

There were no more spots *anywhere* —
Anywhere he looked.

But there *was* a small door.
And what do you think he did?

He opened the door
And stepped outside
To see a world . . .

of color.

For Lynn, Doug, Erin, and Bryan

D. D.

For Paul Scott

G. L.

Text copyright © 1992 by Dayle Ann Dodds
Illustrations copyright © 1992 by Giles Laroche

First Edition

Library of Congress Cataloging-in-Publication Data

Dodds, Dayle Ann.
  The color box / by Dayle Ann Dodds ; illustrated by Giles Laroche.
— 1st ed.
        p.   cm.
  Summary: Alexander the monkey finds an ordinary-looking box with a
spot of color inside, through which he journeys to many bright
landscapes of different colors. Each page has a hole revealing the
next color he will find.
  ISBN 0-316-18820-4
  1. Toy and movable books — Specimens.   [1. Color — Fiction.
2. Monkeys — Fiction.   3. Toy and movable books.]   I. Laroche,
Giles, ill.   II. Title.
PZ7.D66285Co   1992
[E] — dc20   90-22158

10 9 8 7 6 5 4 3 2

TWP

Published simultaneously in Canada
by Little, Brown & Company (Canada) Limited

Printed in Singapore